LIFE EDUCATION

It's My Life

Written by
Pete Sanders and Steve Myers
Illustrated by Kevin Faerber

FRANKLIN WATTS
A Division of Grolier Publishing
NEW YORK • LONDON • HONG KONG • SYDNEY
DANBURY, CONNECTICUT

First American Edition 1997 by
Franklin Watts
A Division of Grolier Publishing
Sherman Turnpike
Danbury, CT 06816

10 9 8 7 6 5 4 3 2 1

Sanders, Pete.
    It's my life / Pete Sanders and Steve Myers.
       p. cm. — (Life education)
    Includes index.
    Summary: Discusses how people develop as
individuals and some of the choices they face that help
shape their lives.
    ISBN 0-531-14429-1
    1. Individual differences—Juvenile literature.
2. Individuality—Juvenile literature. 3. Identity
(Psychology)—Juvenile literature. [1. Individuality. 2.
Conduct of life.] I. Myers, Steve. II. Title. III. Series
    BF697.S239 1997
    155.2'2—dc20   96-11878
                                          CIP AC

Edited by: Helen Lanz
Designed by: Sally Boothroyd
Commissioned photography by:
Peter Millard
Illustrations by: Kevin Faerber

Printed in Italy

Acknowledgments:
Commissioned photography by Peter Millard:
cover; title page.
Researched photography: Eye Ubiquitous 11
(both), 19 (P. Seheult), 21 (Sportshoot); John
Walmsley 5; Network 25 (bottom) (M.
Goldwater); Photofusion 16 (D. Montford), 24
(bottom) (P. White); Robert Harding 9, 13;
The Hutchinson Library 14 (K. Rodgers); Rex
Features 24 (top), 25 (top); Tony Stone 17
(T. Codrington); Zefa 27, 29.
Artwork: Cartoon illustrations by Kevin
Faerber throughout.

The publishers wish to acknowledge that the
photographs reproduced in this book have
been posed by models or obtained from
photographic picture agencies.

Franklin Watts and Life Education
International are indebted to Susan Kaplin,
Amanda Friend, Vince Hatton, and Laurie
Noffs for their invaluable help.

Franklin Watts would like to extend their
special thanks to all the actors who appear
in the Life Education books:

Hester Cann   Chloe Parsons
James Ceppi di Lecco   Dipali Patel
James Chandler

'Each second we live is a new and unique moment of the universe, a moment
that will never be again...And what do we teach our children? We teach
them that two and two make four and that Paris is the capital of France.

When will we also teach them: do you know who you are? You are a marvel.
You are unique. In all the years that have passed, there has never been
another child like you. And look at your body – what a wonder it is! Your
legs, your arms, your clever fingers, the way you move. You may become a
Shakespeare, a Michelangelo, a Beethoven. You have the capacity for
anything. Yes, you are a marvel. And when you grow up, can you then harm
another who is, like you, a marvel? You must cherish one another. You must
work – we must all work – to make this world worthy of its children.'

Pablo Casals

A famous Spanish musician, also noted for his humanitarian beliefs.

(1876 - 1973)

CONTENTS

Get ready to use your brains and expand your minds. We're going to look at YOU in the world.

ONE AND ONLY

Who are you? Sounds like a simple question doesn't it? Most people would probably reply by giving their name. But names are not always unique, whereas people are. So what is it that makes you you? Is it the way you look? Is it how many friends you have? Is it how fast you can run? Is it your family background? The answer is "yes" to all of the above — and much, much more!

ALL YOUR OWN WORK!

Your body is made in such a way that no other person is exactly like you. Individuality, though, is about more than physical differences. It is developed through such things as building up your own knowledge, understanding concepts and ideas, and developing skills. These, in turn, help you to form values and attitudes toward issues that affect you and the world around you.

THE DONE THING

A skill is an ability to do something. Since birth, you have been learning new skills — recognizing people, learning to crawl, walk, talk, read, and so on. Skills are not only physical. Getting along with people, using humor, and being able to make sensible, informed decisions: these, too, are skills that you use many times a day.

STRIKING AN ATTITUDE

Attitudes determine the way you respond to, or feel about, an issue, situation or person. If you dislike someone, your attitude may be hostile. If you love someone, you may be caring and forgiving, even when you yourself are being treated unfairly.

VALUE ADDED FACTS

Attitudes are often based on values, principles or beliefs that we hold. If you have a strong sense that an action is wrong, this will affect your attitude toward anyone doing it. People's values are often different. Two people considering the same facts about a situation may form different attitudes toward it.

Let's get something to eat. I'm starving. I want a GigoBite with everything.

Not here guys — they only sell burgers and hot dogs. They taste lousy and they're nothing but fat and additives. Anyway, Beth's vegetarian.

She's just fussy. How can you not eat meat?

I used to until I found out how they treat some of the animals. Now I don't eat meat on principle. There's another place down the road that serves a bigger variety of stuff. Why don't we all go there?

WHAT'S THE IDEA?

How do we form our ideas? Look at this. We all know that an apple is an apple — but it is also a fruit. In fact it is one of many different kinds of fruit which make up the whole "concept" or "idea" of fruit. Following the same train of thought, an individual act of kindness can be judged by itself, or it can be seen as part of the wider "concept" of love. However, although we can see examples of loving behavior, it is hard to say exactly what love itself is — it does not have a concrete form in the same way that fruit has. It is a concept that we learn about through example.

Home life, watching TV, talking with friends...
What we do and who we mix with influence our lives.

FOR ALL YOU KNOW

Knowledge is all the facts and information which you possess. Your brain collects, stores, and processes huge amounts of material. It takes in whatever data it is given. Your job is to use your brain to make sense of facts — to decide what is true or false, right or wrong. It is vital to be able to make links, and use what you know to understand new information.

CONCERNING YOU

Joey and I have been friends since we were kids. We did everything together and he's a great laugh. I've decided I want to be a doctor and that means I'm going to have to study a lot. Joey says it's a waste of time. He makes fun of me when I have to do homework. I want to stay friends with Joey, but I really want to do well in school. SAM

Dear Sam, Good friendships are important, but so is developing your own ideas. You have to make up your own mind about what is best for you, and about how you handle the opinions of others. Perhaps Joey hasn't yet decided what he wants to do. Doing well in school, though, is not a "waste of time." The more knowledge you have, and the more you have formed your own attitudes, the larger the number of opportunities available to you is likely to be. Good luck!

Why do you think Joey is trying to make Sam feel bad about wanting to study? What would you say to Joey if you were Sam? I know what I'd say.

CHANGING ROOM

Life is about change. Nobody stays exactly the same. You only have to look at the growing process you have already gone through from being a tiny baby to the person you are now to understand this. But physical changes are not the only ones you experience. Your moods, feelings, attitudes, and situations will all alter from time to time. Accepting these changes is not always easy.

SMALL CHANGE

The changes we are most aware of are the ones which have a major, sudden effect on our lives. Many of the changes we go through, however, take place gradually — often over a long period of time.

Or else they may have only a minor influence on us. Sometimes we may not even realize that anything is happening until afterward.

What television program do you watch most / least often?
What do you like to read?
Who is your best friend?
Where do you live?

How tall are you?
How much do you weigh?
What is your favorite color?

What is your favorite food?
What do you do in a normal day?

What is your favorite subject at school?
What clothes do you like to wear?

What kind of music do you like / dislike?

THE WAY WE WERE

Find your current age on the ladder, and write the answers to the questions above on a plain sheet of paper:

Now pick another number from the ladder, lower than your present age. Try answering the same questions, thinking about how you were at that age.

Do the same thing for two or three more ages. If you can't remember exactly what you were like at any particular age, ask people who knew you — your parents or older friends, for instance. When you have done this, compare your answers, and see how your body, likes and dislikes have changed over the years.

FAST FORWARD

Can you do the same thing for future years? Pick a number from above your current "rung" on the ladder. Try to imagine how you think your tastes might change. What changes do you think you might still go through? What about ten or fifteen years after that? Again, if you can't quite imagine any changes, try asking some people who are older than you how their lives have changed.

Who is your favorite singer or band? What career do you want to pursue?

Age 25

Age 24

Age 23

Age 22

Age 21

Age 20

Age 19

Age 18

Age 17

Age 16

15

Age 14

3

What is your favorite sport?

I can't believe that six months ago I didn't want to come here. It was hard at first, but I've made lots of new friends.

I don't want to move. All my friends are here. I won't get to see them anymore. I'll have to go to a new school, and I won't know anybody.

What are the main events in the news that you are aware of?

ADJUSTING YOUR SET-UP

How you react to change will depend on the change itself and the circumstances surrounding it. Changes that you *want* to make are usually easier to adjust to than changes that are outside your control.

Many changes, though, have positive aspects, however upsetting they may seem at the time. The most important thing is to understand the process of change and find out exactly what will be involved. In this way, you can at least be prepared.

Jen's my friend. I don't want to upset her, but I really don't want to go along with this. Trouble is, I'm scared she won't be my friend anymore if I don't.

I'm glad I refused to go along with Jen. She was really horrible about it — it made me realize I don't need friends like her! Sally's a true friend. She doesn't try to make me do things I'm unhappy about.

If you have any worries or concerns about changes you are going through, talking to someone you trust can help.

FEELING YOUR WAY

Everybody has feelings — we'd all be pretty boring human beings if we didn't. The way you feel often affects how you react in any given situation. It's not always easy, though, to make sense of your emotions. Sometimes they take you by surprise, and some can be so strong that they seem to blot out everything else. That's why learning how to handle and express your feelings appropriately is an important part of life.

EMOTE CONTROL

How are you feeling right at this moment? Can you describe why? Often emotions are difficult to put into words. Many also have different intensities, as you can see by looking at the "happy" and "angry" lists opposite. Knowing the kinds of people and situations that make you feel a certain way can help you understand how to express, or control, your feelings when the need arises.

happy:

overjoyed	confident
delighted	worried
proud	scared
cheerful	uncomfortable
content	lonely
	determined

angry:

furious	ashamed
stern	excited
resentful	jealous
indignant	bored
irritated	frustrated
peeved	pleased
depressed	

WHO?   WHY?
WHAT? WHEN?
WHERE? HOW?

GETTING THE FEEL OF IT

Let's take a trip through your emotions. Pick a feeling from the list above, and answer the questions. For instance, if you choose "worried," think about WHAT and WHO worries you, then identify WHY this is the case. HOW do these things and people make you worried? WHEN and WHERE is the feeling most intense? You can use the questions in other ways, especially if the feeling is one you're not happy about. You could ask yourself HOW can you take steps to avoid being with the person or in the situation, or WHO can you talk to about your worries? Try thinking up other words to describe different feelings.

MIXED FEELINGS

To make matters worse, you can have all sorts of emotions going on at the same time. How do you think Sahid and Ellie are feeling?

In fact, Sahid is very happy and Ellie is very sad.

CONCERNING YOU

Sometimes I wake up feeling happy about the day, and by the time I'm eating breakfast I feel as though my dog just died. The smallest things upset me. Mom and Dad don't seem to understand how I feel — I don't know myself half the time. What's going on? SANDRA

Dear Sandra. Unfortunately, moods can be just like a rollercoaster ride — up one minute and down the next. Mood swings are especially common when people are going through puberty. Hormone production in the body is on overtime during this period, and hormones have a particularly strong influence on your emotions. Although they are frustrating, these changes of mood are perfectly natural.

A mood is a strong emotion or combination of emotions that influences the way you act or feel about a situation. A mood can affect other feelings as well. If you're irritable, for instance, you might not feel particularly angry, but would respond angrily to events that you would normally take in stride. If you feel depressed, news which would usually make you happy may have no effect, or perhaps cause you to be even more sad.

Sahid's father has just received an award. Sahid is really happy for him. At the same time, he wishes his mom were still alive to see this.

Ellie has just come from her grandmother's funeral. She is feeling sad about her grandmother's death, but is remembering some of the funny stories she used to tell.

Being depressed or stressed-out can actually affect your general health. If you cannot shake off negative or unhappy feelings, talk to a friend.

FAMILY TIES

Every person is a unique individual — but nobody exists alone. We are constantly in contact with other people throughout our lives. For most of us, the first ones we become aware of are those who make up our family. It is through them that we begin to develop an understanding of who we are and where we fit in in the world.

FAMILY VALUES

Your attitudes, values, and beliefs are determined by several factors. Outside influences, your own experiences and the people you mix with all play a part. However, as you grow up, it is your close relatives who are largely responsible for helping you to develop your responses toward people and issues. It is they who first tell you what is right and wrong, and it is natural for young people initially to adopt their parents' system of values. Sometimes, it may happen without your even realizing it.

Patrick, you've taken that without paying for it, haven't you?

So what? It's only a candy bar. They'll never miss it.

My dad says it's companies like that one who are doing the stealing. Have you seen the prices they charge?

That doesn't mean it's okay to take stuff from them. I've always been brought up to believe that stealing's wrong.

Me too. My family's never really been religious, like Samir's — but they've always taught me to respect other people's property.

ALL IN THE FAMILY

Family does not always mean the same thing to everyone, and not every family situation is identical. The size of families can vary, and some may be very close, whereas others are not. Some young people live with both parents, others may live as part of a one-parent family, either because a parent has died, or as a result of divorce or separation. Some have been adopted or live with step-parents and stepbrothers and sisters.

HOME IMPROVEMENTS

You don't have the choice of the people who make up your family. They are there whether you like it or not! It can often be tempting to look at friends' families and compare them with your own, believing that your situation would be improved if your family were similar to theirs. In most instances this is unlikely to be the case: the grass isn't always greener somewhere else!

Dad's so strict. I don't have any privacy. He's always asking questions about where I'm going, what I'm doing. I wish I lived at Alex's house. His parents are great. They let him do what he wants.

Sometimes I feel like Mom and Dad don't care about anything I do. They never ask me about my friends or anything I've done. I wish I lived with Mark's family. His parents always seem so interested in him.

UNTIL FURTHER NOTICE

Sometimes, brothers and sisters may vie for the attention of their parents. If your mom or dad seems to be choosing a favorite, it can feel very unfair — especially when you're the one who isn't getting the attention! If you have any such worries, talking about them and letting people know how you feel can help to improve the situation.

Well, I've often wondered what it would have been like to have had parents who weren't micro-chips! But I love them all the same, even though they are so *rational* all the time...

CONCERNING YOU

My parents are so old-fashioned. They moan about the way I dress, the music I like — even some of the friends I've made. As far as they're concerned wanting to have pierced ears is a sign of brain damage! I have to be in by nine-thirty, even on weekends, and dad insists on picking me up from the youth group. It's so embarrassing. TANYA.

Dear Tanya, Most young people growing up experience clashes of attitudes with their parents. While you're busy developing your own identity, your parents probably feel as though a stranger is in the house who looks suspiciously like you! Remember, though, that your parents are concerned, not because they don't want you to have a good time, but because they care about you. Why not talk to them calmly about how you feel? Together you might be able to find a way of pleasing everyone.

THAT'S WHAT FRIENDS ARE FOR

Friendships are incredibly important to most of us, whether we choose to have a whole host of friends or just one or two people to whom we are close. As with all relationships, making friends should not only be about looking at what other people have to offer. You're a very special individual. Your friendship is just as valuable to other people as theirs is to you.

CIRCLE OF FRIENDS

We make friends for a variety of reasons. Different friends can fulfill different personal needs. This is Philip and some of his friends.

Fran never minds helping me out if I'm having problems with my homework.

I've been friends with Phil since we were kids. He's lots of fun.

I've known Shereen for years. We go everywhere together.

Shereen and I have lived next door to each other for ages. We often go out together.

I like Rachel — she tells really interesting stories.

I've only known Jessie a short while, but we get along so well, it's like we've been friends forever.

Phil's great to be with! He always makes me laugh.

Jessie's a good friend. If I talk to her about my problems, she always listens.

Fran's my friend because we like doing the same kinds of things together.

Rachel's such a kind person, you can't help but like her!

I don't know where I'd be without my friends — we have a great time surfing the Internet together!

These are only some of the ways in which these people are friends. There are many other [...] between them — and there are many other things that they may discover and like about each other as time goes on.

FRIENDLY PERSUASION

If someone you don't like or trust is asking you to do something you don't feel happy about, it is easy to refuse. If it's a friend who's trying to make you do something you don't want to do, it can be much more difficult to say no. To make it even worse, most people don't just ask once and then stop if you do say no. They will use various techniques to persuade you to agree. Sometimes these methods are not very fair.

This is why it's vital to believe in yourself and stick to what you decide. A true friend will not try to make you do anything you don't want to. Using friendship to manipulate someone into going along with something is unfair.

Speech bubbles: "I thought we were friends." "You'd do it if you cared about me." "I'm your friend — trust me." "You're obviously not a real friend." "Go on — for me." "If you don't, I won't be your friend anymore." "I thought I could rely on you." "None of my other friends refused."

Your friends can make good times even better!

CONCERNING YOU

Jenny and I have known each other since we were five years old, and we've always been great friends. She's angry with me because I've become friendly with Erica, another girl at school. Jenny says that you can't have more than one best friend, and I have to choose between her and Erica. That doesn't seem fair to me. I still want to be friends with Jenny, but I don't want to lose my new friend. SHAHNAZ

Dear Shahnaz, I think you're absolutely right! Of course it's possible to have more than one really good friend. The idea of having a 'best' friend isn't always helpful. It implies that one friendship is more important than another when, in fact, some relationships are equally important. It sounds as if Jenny is a little jealous of Erica — and probably feeling very insecure! Try talking to her. Let her know that your friendship with Erica makes no difference to your friendship with her. Perhaps the three of you could even be friends.

DECISIONS, DECISIONS

How many decisions have you made today? The answer is probably more than you think. Life doesn't just happen around you, and from the moment you get up in the morning to when you go to bed at night, you are constantly making choices and decisions. Some you make almost without thinking. Others may need careful thought. The ability to make sensible, informed decisions is vital.

CONVENTIONAL WISDOM

People often make assumptions without having all the information at their fingertips. It is human nature and unfortunately human nature isn't always helpful. In fact, the more information you have, if possible from a variety of sources, the better able you will be to weigh all the issues. Sometimes, of course, you will have to consider conflicting viewpoints. In such cases, it is important to think through all the options

extra carefully. You will then know you made the best decision you could, even if the outcome wasn't quite as you had hoped.

Discussing views and listening to others can help with the decision-making process.

Did you know that you cannot come to sensible decisions — or be sure that the choice you are making is the one you really want — when you are drunk, stoned, or high?

BORED GAME

Sometimes decisions are made for the wrong reasons. Many young people want to try new things, or are looking for excitement. They may want to be seen as rebels. Some have allowed those kinds of thoughts to cloud their judgment and have taken risks. This can be very dangerous.

A WISE DECISION

Self-esteem means feeling good about yourself and believing in your right to establish your own attitudes and values. It also involves looking after your whole self, both physically and emotionally. Consideration of the following can help when approaching the decision-making PROCESS.

Pressure:

Are other people trying to persuade you to make a decision that you are not happy about? Recognizing the ways in which people try to manipulate you will help you to handle them.

Risk:

Might any part of your decision involve putting yourself at risk? Could you be damaging your health — or harming your friendships? Are the risks really worthwhile?

Overview:

Do you know all you need to know? Where can you get more information? Do you need to talk to anyone else before you decide? Do you have a full picture of the pros and cons of your decision?

Consequence:

What are the possible results of your decision? Think both in terms of the immediate effects and long-term outcomes. Don't only think about yourself. Who else might your decision affect?

Expression:

How do you feel about the situation? Let people know if you are unsure or want more information. If people are putting pressure on you, there are techniques you can use to resist this (see pages 18-19).

Speed:

Do you need to decide right away? Often wrong decisions are made because people make up their minds too quickly. Don't be forced into making an immediate decision if you are unsure or worried about the outcome. If you need time to think, say so.

Self:

Finally, think about yourself. You're a complex human being, with your own thoughts and attitudes. If you know that you do not want to make a decision that might be harmful to your health or self-esteem, you don't have to.

SELLING YOURSELF SHORT

Advertisements are everywhere. You can't walk down the street, turn on the TV, or read a magazine without being bombarded with words and images. All of the advertisements around you are trying to persuade you to use a particular product, buy one brand of goods instead of another, or think in a certain way.

THE WHOLE TRUTH

"Cholesterol Heaven! Apples are cheaper, though, and much better for you."

Have you noticed how you never see advertisements like these? Ads are there to sell you a product or idea. Although they're not permitted to be deliberately misleading, they don't have to tell you everything about what they are selling.

MIXED MESSAGES

Making sense of the messages ads put across is not always simple. It's easy to get carried away by the power of advertising. Geoff is getting ready to go out.

He's decided that to impress the girls, he needs to smell good. He's seen the ads and knows just what to use. Or so he thinks:

Maybe I've overdone it slightly. They smelled great on their own. Together they make me smell like a ripe Gorgonzola!

THE LABEL STABLE

Advertising is big business, and nowhere is this more evident than in the world of the designer label. Show some people an ordinary, inexpensive T-shirt and they'll say they wouldn't be seen dead in it. Show them the same T-shirt, with a designer logo the size of a pin-head and a price tag ten times higher than the first, and they'll decide that life isn't worth living unless they own it!

What influences the choices you make?

BARGAIN BASEMENT

Sounds like a bargain! There's just one problem. What exactly is it? Do you plug it in, drink it, spread it on your legs? Finding out precisely what you are buying is vital. Official advertisements don't always tell you everything. Unofficial ones — or people who are trying to get you to go along with something — may make outrageous claims or even tell outright lies to try to persuade you.

Hi, Ned, looking good!

Thanks, Bill. It's the latest stuff. Cost me a fortune.

He looks a bit weird, actually. Why is he wearing all that stuff on a day like this?

I'm so hot. I'd love to take this jacket off, but it would spoil the effect. Why am I putting myself through this? Bill looks much more comfortable.

Look at you two. What happened? Nobody wears that kind of stuff anymore. You need designer stuff to look good.

I don't as a matter of fact. This is precisely what everybody is still wearing. It's the clothes you're all wearing which are going to look out of date in a month.

You just don't understand fashion.

We understand it well enough to know that you're just following a trend. We're setting one — a no designer label trend. And that's really the latest fashion statement! Come on, Gita, let's go.

According to my data, ads can be used to make people think things like smoking or drinking lots of alcohol are macho or trendy, when really they are no good for you at all.

RESPONSE ABILITY

You know how it is. You've made up your mind and know exactly what you want to say. Then when it comes to saying it, it's as if someone else is working your mouth! The words come out wrong, or you find yourself agreeing to things when you don't want to. The good news is that there are ways to make sure that you say what you mean to say. The technique of making sure you get your message across is called "assertiveness."

SPEAK YOUR MIND

Instead of having stated exactly how she feels, Teresa has now left herself open to further persuasion from Pam.

The first rule of speaking your mind is just that — say what you feel. If you don't want to do something, don't say "I don't know" or "We-ell" or "I'm not sure." Start by saying "I don't want to do that." Then if you can say nothing else, at least you've voiced a clear opinion.

REPEAT PERFORMANCE

You know how annoying it can be when a record or CD sticks and the same sequence plays over and over. This kind of repetition can be a useful strategy when someone is trying to persuade you to do something which you know is wrong or don't want to do. It works as you'd expect, by repeating your answer or reason several times. It's important to use the same words and not go into too much detail. Speak clearly and calmly, without raising your voice.

DISARMAMENT TREATY

People who want to upset you or make you look foolish in front of others may use insults or try to humiliate you. They might make negative remarks about the way you dress or about your family. These can be hard to listen to. You may feel like lashing out physically or verbally at the other person, or being nasty back. Far more effective is the disarming technique:

> Look who it is. You look awful — that shirt is so strange.

> Yes, it is unusual, isn't it? Then again, I think fashion's a matter of personal choice.

By appearing to agree with the insult, Teresa has taken the power out of it and confused Pam, while maintaining her own dignity.

CONCERNING YOU

A group of us at school hang around together. It's fun, but lately some of my friends have started to dare each other. Now they're stealing from shops and taking stupid risks. I don't like it, and someone could be hurt. I've tried to say something, but I'm shouted down or ignored. I don't want to lose my friends, but I don't want any part of this. Help! FARIBA

Dear Fariba, Being in a group can be fun, but sometimes gang members go along with things they know are wrong. Speaking out is difficult, especially if you are the only one doing so. Most people worth being friends with, though, will know that stealing is wrong. I'm sure that in the long run they will admire you for sticking up for yourself. However, if you are continually thinking in a different way from your group, it may be time to find other friends who think more like you do.

I SAY, I SAY, I SAY

Another tip is to use "I" instead of "You" to make your answer forceful but not aggressive. If you say "You're always late," you might get the response "No, I'm not," and you are immediately in a conflict. If you were to say "I feel upset because I've been waiting a long time," that would be an assertive response, and the other person can't say "No you're not upset..." in reply.

You may need to practice what to say in awkward situations more than I do — but at least nobody can come along and just switch you off! Imagine how frustrating *that* is!!

Most products come with a full set of instructions for use and give you all the necessary details you need to look after them. The human body has no such instruction book. It's up to you to learn how the body functions, what helps it work well, and what you can do to make sure it keeps on working at its best.

MAN & MACHINE

The human body has often been compared to a living machine.

① air intake
② fuel intake
③ fuel tank
④ control panel and electrical circuitry
⑤ safety cage

Both need regular cleaning and exercising and both require careful "driving." They rely on their owners for the right fuel. If you put the wrong kind of gas in a car, it will not run so well. The same is true of your body. With the right fuel, your body will give you peak performance.

ROAD TO NOWHERE

As you go through life, you will have to make decisions about many different possibilities, opportunities, and temptations. Wayne is not sure which road to take. The one ahead looks unexciting: there are dark clouds up ahead and he's been on this road for quite a while now. It would be simple to take one of the turnoffs. He can't see far down these roads, but they all look better than the one he's on. Why shouldn't he follow one of these? Well, sometimes the most tempting routes are not the best ones.

LOOKING FORWARD TO IT

It can be frustrating if you have to wait before you can do something you're excited about. Yet looking forward to things can actually make them more fulfilling. Part of the fun of holidays is thinking about what you're going to do and making plans. Growing up can be exciting too. It may seem like a slow process, but rushing it or skipping stages is like making a pie without putting in a filling — it's all pastry! The satisfying, tasty part in the middle just isn't there!

Top athlete or not? Looking after your body helps to give you the best chances in life!

SOONER OR LATER

Temptations can be hard to resist — that's why they're called temptations, after all! Often it's easy to see only the immediate effects of a decision. However, thinking about the long-term consequences of your actions can help you avoid making decisions that at first seem like a good idea, but that you later end up regretting.

Hey, it's fun leaping forward and seeing what will happen next! It's OK for me, though, because I can easily go back to see what I have missed. You humans need to make sure you were there the first time around.

FOR BETTER, FOR WORSE

Drugs work by altering or interfering with a particular process in the body. Most people will take a medicinal drug at some point in their lives, to help them get over an illness. Used correctly to treat certain medical conditions, they can be beneficial. Used incorrectly, they can have devastating effects on a person's life.

DRUG USE:
Taking a drug for its correct medical purpose in the right amount at the right times and by the proper method.

DRUG MISUSE:
Taking a drug for the correct purpose, but using it too frequently, taking too much of it, or taking it in the wrong way.

DRUG ABUSE:
Taking a drug for a reason other than to treat a medical condition and in such a manner or frequency that damage can be caused to a person's health.

ONLY MAKE BELIEVE

People often misuse or abuse drugs because they believe it will make them feel good, or will help them perform in a particular situation. In fact, far from being beneficial, drug abuse damages not only people's health, but also their self-esteem. Because many drugs are addictive, drug abusers forget about everything else that might matter to them, including their relationships with other people and their own well-being. It's just not worth it.

WHAT'S IN IT FOR YOU?

I've got some top-quality brick dust.

I've got the finest talcum powder on the market.

Vets use this to stun elephants.

What would you say if someone asked you to eat or drink any of these? A resounding no to every one of them, hopefully. People who buy and use drugs illegally can never be certain exactly what they are getting. Many drugs are poisonous in their pure form and have to be mixed with other substances before they can be used. Suppliers are not usually bothered by what substances they choose, and people have indeed taken drugs containing brick dust and talcum powder.

SURPRISE, SURPRISE!

If you are prescribed a drug by a doctor or buy one from a pharmacist, you will be given clear instructions about the strength of the drug and the correct dosage. Illegally bought drugs carry no such instructions. Some drugs have added ingredients, while drugs that are too pure cause severe health problems, sometimes even death. A drug abuser can never be sure of the strength of the drug he or she is taking, and cannot therefore safely predict the effect it will have. Even buying from the same person every time is no guarantee. Suppliers may not know themselves exactly what they are selling.

They're only steroids, Rashid. They'll make you run faster and be stronger. It's more dangerous crossing the road than taking this stuff.

That's like lying down in the road and hoping the traffic won't hit you! Those things are dangerous — and illegal.

They can cause all sorts of side effects — heart disease, cancer — people have even died from taking them.

Don't be stupid. My mom took steroids once after she'd been in the hospital.

But they were prescribed for her for a specific reason. These are from a friend of a friend of a friend. You don't even know for sure what they are. Count me out.

Rashid's right. I thought it was cool, but it's just stupid. I don't need drugs to have fun.

CONCERNING YOU

A while back, my dad had a throat infection, and the doctor prescribed some tablets for him. He took most of them, but there were still a few left. Now my mom has a bad throat, and she says it's not worth going to the doctor. She says she can take the tablets my dad didn't use because it's the same kind of infection. I don't think that's right. BREDA

Dear Breda, You're quite correct. Taking a medicine that was prescribed for someone else, even if you think you have the same symptoms, can be very dangerous. Doctors don't only prescribe a certain drug for a particular illness; they take into account the person who is ill and prescribe the most suitable medicine for both the condition and the person. Someone else taking the drug might experience very different, even damaging, results.

The human mind is so wonderful — why harm it with drugs? I envy you with your capacity for seeing, hearing, feeling.... Living life to the full means looking after what you've got!

23

WELL, WHAT DO YOU KNOW?

Your body is a finely balanced series of systems, all working together. It's important to remember that the way you treat it and everything you put inside it will have an effect on how well it works. Young people often have their own ideas about drugs, many of which are far from the truth. Here are just a few of the things people say:

Drugs are only harmful if you inject them.

!!! All misused drugs, whether sniffed, swallowed, smoked or injected, are harmful. Injecting prescribed, medicinal drugs, such as insulin, is usually done cleanly and safely as part of a proper routine. Injecting illegal drugs, however, is especially dangerous because the drug is introduced directly into the bloodstream. Sharing needles can also increase the risk of contracting HIV.

Do you __need__ to drink or smoke to have a good time?

Smoking and drinking alcohol are legal so they can't really be dangerous.

Drug "paraphenalia" – looks scary, doesn't it?

Soft drugs like marijuana won't do any damage. It's only the hard drugs, like cocaine, that are dangerous.

!!! Not true. Any drug can be dangerous. The labels "soft" and "hard" are inaccurate because they imply that one is safer than another. Marijuana has many health risks for the body. Among other things, it damages the lungs, can become addictive, cause memory disorders and affects the immune system.

!!! Smoking and drinking are much more harmful to young people who are still growing than to adults. Adults are expected to make responsible decisions about their tobacco and alcohol use. Unfortunately, not all adults act so responsibly and some didn't know of the damaging effects of smoking before they started. More people die each year from the effects of tobacco and alcohol than from other forms of drug abuse.

> Smoking one or two cigarettes a day won't do me any harm.

!!! There are many substances contained in cigarette smoke, some of them poisonous. Nicotine, one of the main ones, is also very addictive. There are extremely few people who manage to stick to one or two cigarettes a day.

> I can try drugs once. I'll be able to stop if I don't like them.

!!! Some drugs are addictive after the first use. What's more, misusing drugs even once can be dangerous. For instance, people have died after taking just one Ecstasy tablet. On top of all this, since many drugs alter your mood or behavior, you may not be able to reason clearly enough to decide not to take the drug a second time.

> My granpa's been smoking for years, and he's okay!

!!! Among other things, smoking can cause high blood pressure, heart disease, cancer of the lungs and other organs, bronchitis, and emphysema. Many smokers die prematurely as a result of their tobacco use. It's true that some do live to an old age, but they may still have chronic medical problems.

> Not all drugs are addictive.

!!! Addiction is difficult to measure, and all drugs have the potential to be addictive. Even if the body does not crave the drug, a person can still be addicted to the effects that the drug has on the brain.

The actor, River Phoenix, died from the results of drug abuse.

> Drinking alcohol makes you grown up and sophisticated.

!!! There is no such thing as a sophisticated drunk! Think of how silly or aggressive people can get after drinking alcohol.

Drug rehabilitation centers aim to help people overcome drug addiction.

> All those things to remember! Actually, it all just boils down to one point: look after yourself and give your body its best chance. But remember, if you are confused or concerned in any way, speak to someone you trust.

ALL TOGETHER NOW

As individuals we expect other people to respect us. Other people, however, also expect *us* to respect *them*. This is only fair, and shows us how important it is to act in a responsible and considerate way.

ME, MYSELF, I

If you go through life like Matthew, ignoring pleas for the help and support you yourself will need from time to time, it should come as no surprise if friends eventually decide that you don't deserve their attention. We all have a collective responsibility toward each other. What's more, talking through a problem with a friend, or devoting time and energy to issues that do not concern us directly, but that help others, can be very rewarding.

YOU CAN'T LOSE

From time to time, we all experience situations in which we are in disagreement with another person. The trick to handling these is to try to find solutions that satisfy both parties. If you just stubbornly refuse to budge from your position, you are unlikely to be able to solve your differences. This doesn't mean that you always have to give in, but it does mean being prepared to consider all the options, and perhaps meeting people halfway sometimes.

STOCK TAKE

Everyone has strengths and weaknesses. Recognizing this is often the first step to living to your full potential. It's worth spending a few minutes thinking about the things you're good at, and then about the areas you would like to improve. Be brutally honest with yourself — nobody else is going to know! Think through everything, however unimportant some points might seem. The next step is to consider practical ways in which you can work on your strengths to make them even better. Finally, look at your weaknesses. Is there a way to turn them into strengths?

CONCERNING YOU

I have several friends at school that I hang around with. We all know each other well and get along together. Lately, though, they've started to make fun of this other kid who tried to make friends with us. She's nervous and shy — not like the others. I don't think it's fair to pick on her just because she's different. NATALIE

Dear Natalie: You're right. It isn't fair. Every person is different from everyone else — in one way or another. Focusing on that as the sole reason for disliking someone smacks of discrimination and prejudice. Each of us has something to offer. If your friends concentrated on this girl's strengths, instead of making jokes about what they see as weaknesses, they might be pleasantly surprised.

Not only do we look different but we _are_ different! We all have different strengths and weaknesses, hopes and dreams. This can be a very good thing!

As I flip through my History-of-Human-Beings CDs, it's clear that human behavior changes from time to time, culture to culture. I particularly like the way in which you can be kind towards each other.

27

THE FUTURE STARTS HERE

Your body needs balance in order to work efficiently. This kind of balance can be seen throughout life. Just as every cell has a function in a particular body, societies need to have structure and order. This same harmony occurs on a wider planetary scale, with every living thing playing its special role in what is known as the "ecosystem."

SCHOOL DAZE

It can be annoying to have to follow certain rules. Most of these, however, are there for a very good reason, even if the reason isn't immediately obvious! Nobody likes to feel restricted, but sometimes a routine is useful. It helps us to know what is expected of us, and when! Rules at school are also there to help us to learn. If you don't pass your exams, how will you find the job you want?

Each person is a special individual with something to offer. Every little bit of good you do makes a huge difference to society.

CONCERNING YOU

I've joined several organizations that are all campaigning for different issues I feel strongly about. Now a friend of mine is pestering me to join another one. It's not that I don't think it's an important issue, it's just that there are so many to think about. I can't do something for every one, can I?
TYRONE

Dear Tyrone, Probably not! It can be confusing as you start to take an interest in issues that affect your life and the lives of other people. The amount of information and the number of messages around is bewildering. I think you are right — you probably have to make the choice of devoting your energies to one or two causes only. If you try to do everything, you will end up being frustrated, feeling as if you did none of it well.

A DROP IN THE OCEAN

When you think of yourself in terms of the whole planet, it can be easy to be overwhelmed. All those millions of people living their lives - do you really count at all? The answer, of course, is a gigantic YES, YOU DO. A pebble thrown in a pond makes a large pattern of ripples. Even seemingly insignificant actions can have wide-ranging effects.

THE DIFFERENCE IS YOU

As you go through life, it's important to remember that we can all make a difference to the people and places around us. Whatever you decide to do with your life, remember that your attitudes, thoughts, ideas, and values are worthwhile. Develop them with care and cherish them! It's your life. Have fun — and make a difference!

LETTER FROM LIFE EDUCATION

Dear Friends:

The first Life Education Center was opened in Sydney, Australia, in 1979. Founded by the Rev. Ted Noffs, the Life Education program came about as a result of his many years of work with drug addicts and their families. Noffs realized that preventive education, beginning with children from the earliest possible age all the way into their teenage years, was the only long-term solution to drug abuse and other related social problems.

Life Education pioneered the use of technology in a "Classroom of the 21st Century," designed to show how drugs, including nicotine and alcohol, can destroy the delicate balance of human life. In every Life Education classroom, electronic displays show the major body systems, including the respiratory, nervous, digestive and immune systems. There is also a talking brain, a wondrous star ceiling, and Harold the Giraffe, Life Education's official mascot. Programs start in preschool and continue through high school.

Life Education also conducts parents' programs including violence prevention classes, and it has also begun to create interactive software for home and school computers.

There are Life Education Centers operating in seven countries (Thailand, the United States, the United Kingdom, New Zealand, Australia, Hong Kong, and New Guinea), and there is a Life Education home page on the Internet (the address is http://www.lec.org/).

If you would like to learn more about Life Education International contact us at one of the addresses listed below or, if you have a computer with a modem, you can write to Harold the Giraffe at Harold@lec.org and you'll find out that a giraffe can send E-mail!

Let's learn to live.

All of us at the Life Education Center.

Life Education, USA
149 Addison Ave
Elmhurst, Illinois
60126
Tel: 630 530 8999
Fax: 630 530 7241

Life Education, UK
20 Long Lane
London
EC1A 9HL
United Kingdom

Life Education,
Australia
PO Box 1671
Potts Point
NSW 2011
Australia

Life Education,
New Zealand
126 The Terrace
PO Box 10-769
Wellington
New Zealand

GLOSSARY

Abuse To use or treat someone or something in a way that is wrong, often over a considerable period of time and in a way that will cause serious harm.

Assertive Someone who is forthright about what they believe, and is not put off by the opinions or teasing of others. Being assertive does not mean being loud or rude, quiet determination is usually far more effective!

Assumption Something that is taken as being true although there is no immediate proof that it is.

Attitude A way of thinking or behaving.

Cocaine A drug originally made from the coca plant, but now usually made synthetically. It is sometimes used medically as a local anaesthetic; it is also an addictive stimulant.

Concept General idea about a subject. The word usually refers to ideas that are abstract.

Designer label Originally referring to the maker's label sewn into a garment and later to the designer's logo on the garment, the term is now used to describe high fashion (and highly expensive) clothes.

Disarming technique A good way of dealing with someone who is being unpleasant to you: agree with what they say! This could also be called "Taking the wind out of their sails technique." Very

effective, although as the instinctive response is to be nasty back it may require concentration at first!

Emphysema A condition in which the air cells of the lungs become swollen, which in turn, causes breathlessness.

Gorgonzola A type of Italian cheese usually made from cow's milk.

HIV Abbreviation of the term human immunodeficiency virus, the virus which can lead to the development of AIDS.

Immune system The body's defense system against infection of all kinds.

Manipulate Although this can mean using something skillfully, such as a tool, in the context of this book it means trying to use or influence someone unfairly and against their will.

Marijuana A drug made from the dried leaves, flowers and stems of the hemp plant.

Misuse To use someone or something in the wrong way.

Nicotine The chemical in tobacco that is addictive.

Positive This word has different meanings in different contexts. In this book it means someone or something that is constructive, confident, and outward-looking, and probably also assertive.

Prescribe To advise the use of a particular medicine.

Principles Basic truths that are used as a guide to action and behavior by societies, for example that murder is wrong. Some principles can be a matter of individual choice, such as whether or not to be a vegetarian.

Values Another word with several different meanings. In this book it is similar to "principles," meaning standards that are important in life and society as a whole.

FURTHER INFORMATION

These organizations can help you with your questions:

American Humane Association Children's Division
63 Inverness Drive E
Englewood, CO 80112-5117
Tel: (303) 792-9900
    (800) 227-4645

Child Welfare League of America
440 1st Street NW,
Suite 310
Washington, DC 20001
Tel: (202) 638-2952

Committee for Children
2203 Airport Way S,
Suite 500
Seattle, WA 98134-2027
Tel: (206) 343-1223
    (800) 634-4449

Friends of the Earth
1025 Vermont Avenue NW,
3rd Floor
Washington, DC 20005
Tel: (202) 783-7400

INDEX